# Seeds of Love

### For Brothers and Sisters of International Adoption

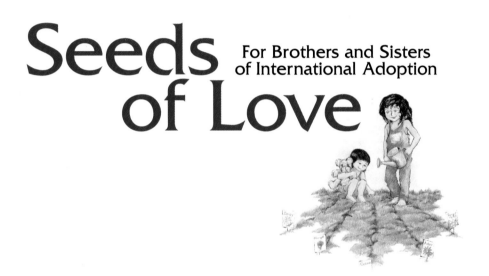

Written by Mary E. Petertyl
Illustrated by Jill Chambers

First Edition
Folio One Publishing, Grand Rapids, Michigan

Text Copyright ©1997 by Mary E. Petertyl
Illustrations Copyright ©1997 by Jill Chambers

Published by **Folio One Publishing**
4519 Cascade Road SE, Grand Rapids, Michigan 49546

Designed by Michele Most-Miller

Printed in Hong Kong

For Dylan, Carly and Anna
— M.E.P.

For Norman and Jenna
— J.C.

For Jennifer and Heather
— M.M.M.

*Publisher's Cataloging-in-Publication*
(Prepared by Quality Books Inc.)

Petertyl, Mary E.
Seeds of love : for brothers and sisters of international adoption / written by Mary E. Petertyl ;
illustrated by Jill Chambers. — 1st ed.
p.        cm.
Summary: Carly works through feelings of anticipation and fear when her parents travel
to another country without her to adopt her baby sister.
Preassigned LCCN: 96-61921
ISBN 0-9655753-1-4
1. Adoption — Juvenile literature. 2. Adopted children — Juvenile literature.
I. Chambers, Jill. II. Title.
HV875.P48  1997        362.7'34        QBI96-40843

# This Book Belongs

To_____

From _____

Date_____

Last year, I became a big sister.

When my mommy first told me about our baby,
I thought about all the great things we would do
together...

I was excited.

And I told my mommy so.

"I'm glad, Carly," she said. "But remember, it will take some time before our baby can do the big-kid things that you like to do. You will have to teach her."

Then Mommy told me something kind of funny. She said our baby was in another country, and that she and Daddy would be going on an airplane to get her.

I didn't know babies came from airplanes.

And I told my mommy so.

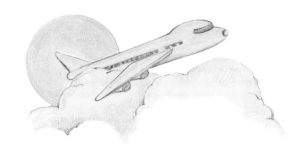

"Oh, honey. Babies don't come from airplanes," she said. "Your sister was born to a mommy, just like you were. But her parents couldn't take care of her, so our family is going to adopt her.

"The airplane will take Daddy and me to her, then bring us back home to you."

Then I wondered, if Mommy and Daddy are going on an airplane to get my baby sister, who is going to stay here with me?

That made me feel scared.

And I told my mommy so.

"Gramma is going to stay with you," she said.
"The two of you will have lots of fun together."

"But how would Gramma know how to take care
of me?" I asked.

"Would she cut the crust from my toast at breakfast?
Would she remember to take me to dance class on
Tuesdays? Would she let me sleep with my night
light on? I can't sleep without my night light."

My mommy said not to worry. Gramma was her
mommy when she was a little girl. She would know
what to do. And if she didn't, I could just tell her.

When the time came for Mommy and Daddy to go, they packed all kinds of stuff, like clothes and shoes and bathroom things, books and magazines, some important-looking papers, a camera, and about a zillion rolls of film.

I wondered if Gramma would bring her camera to take pictures of me, too.

For our baby they packed clothes so little they looked
like they'd fit my doll Lucy, baby wipes, diapers, creams
and powders, and a couple toys that they said I liked
to play with when I was a baby.

I put a picture of me in the suitcase too, so they could
show my baby sister.

Once they were all packed, Mommy took me down
to the kitchen where we keep our family calendar.

"I have marked the days that we will be gone," she
said. "When you wake up in the morning, place a
sticker on that day. Each sticker means we are one
day closer to being together again."

Then she took out a little pot, a packet of seeds, and a small bag of dirt. We planted several of the seeds together.

"Carly," she said. "I want you to keep this pot by a sunny window and water it — just a little — every day. When the plants sprout up, we will be coming home to you very soon."

At the airport, I wasn't feeling very happy. But,
this time, instead of telling Mommy, I showed her.
I started to cry.

"I'm going to miss you," I said. "You're going away
for such a long time."

"It seems like a long time now," she said. "But the
time will go by quickly. Just remember to have fun
with Gramma and take good care of your seeds."

She dried my tears and gave me a hug.
She smelled so nice.

The next morning I jumped out of bed, put a sticker on the calendar, and watered my seeds — just a little.

And you know what? Gramma and I did have lots of fun!

We checked out the baby animal exhibit at the zoo, spent a whole afternoon playing dress-up — with real make-up, and baked thumb-print cookies. Gramma even let me lick the spoon. Mommy never lets me lick the spoon!

One day the phone rang. It was Mommy and Daddy.
They only had a minute to talk, but said they loved
and missed me very much.

They also said that my baby sister was with them, that
she was healthy and beautiful, and they decided to
name her Anna.

But the very best news of all was that they were
coming home soon!

As soon as I hung up the phone, I checked my seeds.
A couple of sprouts had poked up through the dirt!

As my sprouts grew more and more, I missed my parents more and more.

Then one night, when I checked my sprouts, small green leaves had unfolded. It wouldn't be long now!

When the big day came. I put the last sticker on the calendar, watered my little plants, and went to the airport with Gramma.

We were all so very happy to see each other. I had fun with Gramma, but I was glad Mommy and Daddy were home.

I was also glad they brought home my new baby sister. She was even softer and sweeter than I had imagined.

I loved her the moment I saw her.

And I told little Anna so.